Thank you a thousand million times.
For new friendships forged in extraordinary times;
for old friendships that held fast – D.G.

To everyone at Gledhow Primary,
the quiet ones and the chatterboxes! – A.B. x

BLOOMSBURY CHILDREN'S BOOKS
Bloomsbury Publishing Plc
50 Bedford Square, London, WC1B 3DP, UK
29 Earlsfort Terrace, Dublin 2, Ireland

BLOOMSBURY, BLOOMSBURY CHILDREN'S BOOKS and the Diana logo are trademarks of Bloomsbury Publishing Plc
First published in Great Britain 2022 by Bloomsbury Publishing Plc

Text copyright © Debi Gliori 2022
Illustrations copyright © Alison Brown 2022

Debi Gliori and Alison Brown have asserted their rights under the Copyright, Design and Patents Act, 1988,
to be identified as the Author and Illustrator of this work.

ISBN 978-1-5266-2827-5 (HB)
ISBN 978-1-5266-2828-2 (PB)
ISBN 978-1-5266-2826-8 (eBook)

2 4 6 8 10 9 7 5 3 1

Printed in China by Leo Paper Products, Heshan, Guangdong

MIX
Paper from
responsible sources
FSC
www.fsc.org   FSC® C020056

To find out more about our authors and books visit www.bloomsbury.com and sign up for our newsletters

Little Owl's New Friend

Debi Gliori

Alison Brown

BLOOMSBURY
CHILDREN'S BOOKS
LONDON OXFORD NEW YORK NEW DELHI SYDNEY

Little Owl was playing
Feeding-Time-at-the-Zoo with Hedge.
It was Hedge's turn to be the Hungry Lion
and Little Owl was Dinner.

"Come on, Hedge," said Little Owl,
"I can't hear you. Be a proper lion.
Pretend you're about to gobble me up.
Go **RWAAAAR**."

"Oh my goodness!" said Mummy Owl.
"What a scary lion!
Luckily, Small Squirrel has come to play.
She'll rescue you from that hungry lion."

Little Owl looked up.
There was a small Something
holding on to Mummy Owl.

"No!" said Little Owl.

"NO,

NO,

NO!"

"Oh dear," said Mummy Owl.

"NO," said Little Owl,
"I don't want to play
with Small Squirrel.

I want Hedge
to be a lion and go
RWAAARRR
and gobble me up."

Mummy Owl blinked.
"What a pity," she said. "We brought
cinnamon buns to feed your lion,
but if it's not very hungry, we'll give them
to the **bears in the bushes** instead."

Little Owl's eyes grew wide.
Bears? In the bushes?
He ran off to investigate.

Small Squirrel trailed behind.

The cinnamon buns smelled so delicious.
She reached out a paw.
Surely the bears wouldn't mind…

Five buns later, Little Owl
and Small Squirrel were back.
"Mummy!" squeaked Little Owl,
"I can't find those bears anywhere
but Something has eaten the buns!
They've all gone!"

"Really?" said Mummy Owl, staring at Small Squirrel. "Maybe it was a **Snaffle-Worm**. So greedy. They're always popping up at picnics and stealing all the sandwiches. Only the best hunters can find their nest…"

"That's me!
That's what I am!"
interrupted Small Squirrel.
"I'm the best hunter.
My mummy says I'm the
best hunter that ever was.
In the whole forest.
Yes! In fact, I'm the best
in the whole world.
In the universe.

Come on Little Owl!
Come and watch me hunt!
I'll find their nest!
I'll hunt and I'll hunt and
I'll find where they're hiding
and … what are they called again?"

"Snaffle-Worms," sighed Little Owl.
Small Squirrel was making his ears wilt.

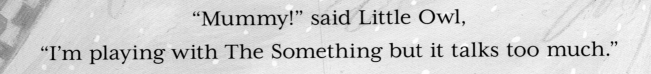

"Mummy!" said Little Owl,
"I'm playing with The Something but it talks too much."

"I heard," said Mummy Owl, pegging washing out to dry.
"Hopefully, the noise will keep the **Hush-Hush** away."

"The **Hush-Hush**?" said Little Owl. "What's that?"
"Oh," said Mummy Owl, "nothing important.
Totally harmless. You probably won't even see it."
"Is it a sort of ghost?" said Little Owl.

"Ghosts don't scare me!"
squeaked Small Squirrel.
"I'll show them!

I'm so brave.
I'm the bravest
Small Squirrel
in the world!
My mummy says ...

What's that thing behind you?"

"It's a GHOST!"
said Little Owl.

"Waaaaaa!
I want my mummy!"
said Small Squirrel.

And she flung herself down on
the ground and began to cry.

Little Owl didn't like to see Small Squirrel crying.
He wrapped his little wings round Small Squirrel
and hugged her tight.

"Don't cry," said Little Owl.
"It's all right. I'm here. I'll protect you.
Look! It's only a sheet, not a ghost after all."

Small Squirrel blinked and nodded. Little Owl was right.
"Small Squirrel," said Little Owl, "I've got a really good idea.
Can you RWAAARRRRRR really loudly?"

"Whoo hoo, RWARRRRRRR!"
said the Hush-Hush,
lurching into the kitchen.

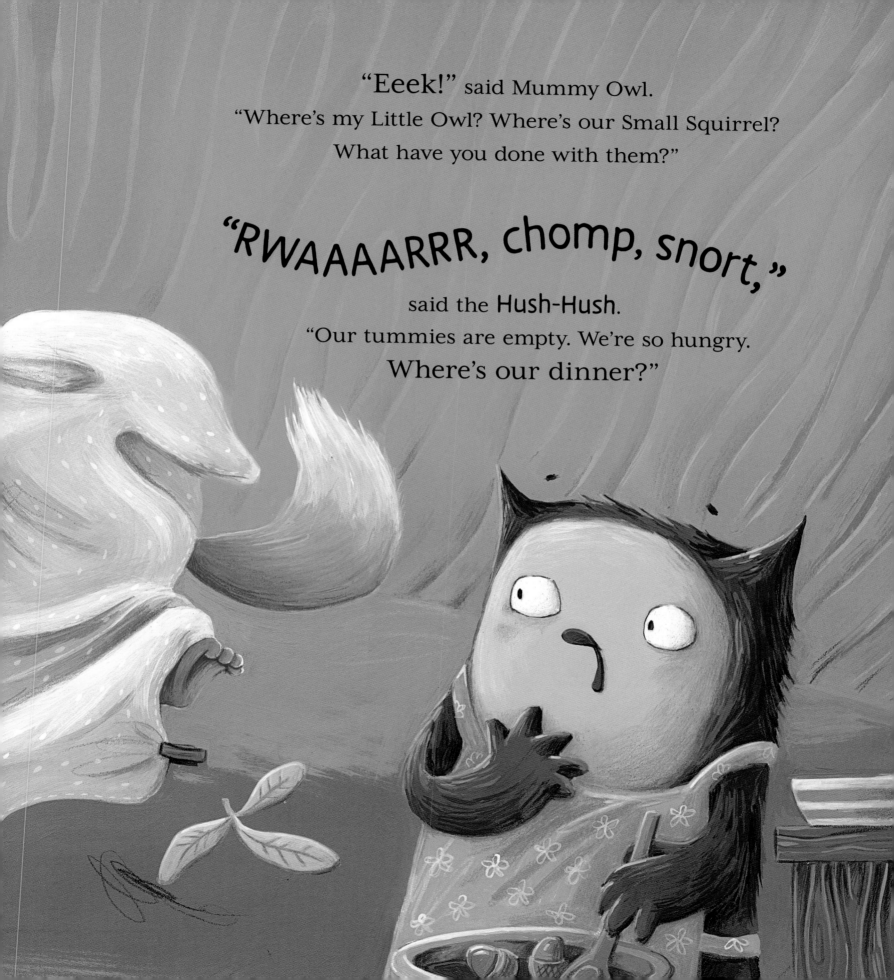

"Eeek!" said Mummy Owl.
"Where's my Little Owl? Where's our Small Squirrel?
What have you done with them?"

"RWAAAARRR, chomp, snort,"

said the Hush-Hush.
"Our tummies are empty. We're so hungry.
Where's our dinner?"

Small Squirrel didn't stop talking
while she ate two bowls of acorn soup,
five seedy crackers and
two and a half slices of hazelnut-cream pie.

After supper,
Small Squirrel's mummy
came to take her home.

As they left, Little Owl could still hear
Small Squirrel talking. Non-stop.

"It's very dark," said Small Squirrel.
"Hold my paw, Mummy.
We saw bears and lions
and there was a Hush-Hush.
Can I go back to visit the Owls again?
Little Owl is my bestest best friend."

"You've made a very talkative new friend!"
said Mummy Owl, tucking Little Owl in.

"Yes..." yawned Little Owl.
"Small Squirrel is so funny.
And she can **RWARRR** like a proper lion.
I hope she comes to play again."

Then at long last, silence fell in the Owl House.
Little Owl hugged his very quiet best friend, Hedge,
and soon he was fast asleep.